To ....

For being good.

MERRY CHRISTMAS!

From Santa

Santa is coming to The Great Smoky Mountains

Written by Steve Smallman
Illustrated by Robert Dunn
Designed by Sarah Allen

Copyright © Hometown World Ltd. 2013

Published by Sourcebooks Jabberwocky, an imprint of Sourcebooks, Inc.
P.O. Box 4410, Naperville, Illinois 60567-4410
(630) 961-3900
Fax: (630) 961-2168
www.jabberwockykids.com

Library of Congress Cataloging-in-Publication data is on file with the publisher.

Source of Production: Leo Paper Products, Guangdong Province, China
Date of Production: April 2014
Run Number: HTW_PO170314
Printed and bound in China
LEO 10 9 8 7 6 5 4 3 2

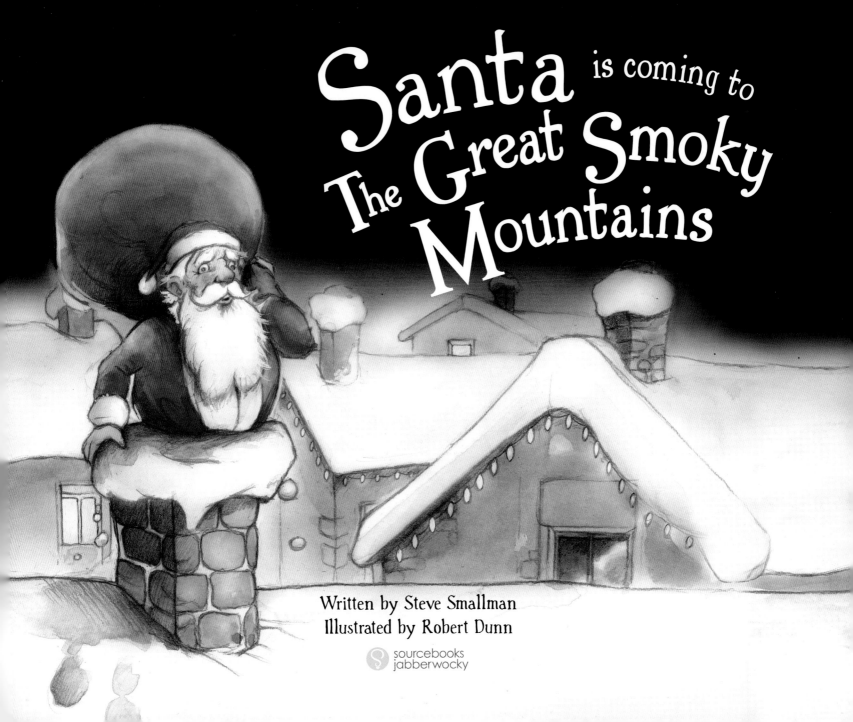

Santa is coming to The Great Smoky Mountains

Written by Steve Smallman
Illustrated by Robert Dunn

sourcebooks
jabberwocky

"Well?"

boomed Santa. "Have all the children from the **Great Smoky Mountains** been good this year?"

"Well...uh...mostly," answered the little old elf, as he bustled across the busy workshop to Santa's desk.

Santa peered down at the elf from behind the tall, teetering piles of letters that the children of the Great Smoky Mountains had sent him.

"Mostly?" asked Santa, looking over the top of his glasses.

"Yes...but they've all been **especially** good in the last few days!" said the elf.

"Jolly good!" chuckled Santa,
"Then we'd better get their presents loaded up!"

Even though the sack of presents was

really, really big

and the elves were **really, really** small,

they seemed to have no trouble loading it onto Santa's sleigh.
Though how they managed to fit such a big sack into one little sleigh
even they didn't know. But somehow they did.

"Splendid!" boomed Santa. "We're ready to go!"

"Er...not quite, Santa," said the little old elf. "One of our reindeer is missing!"

"Missing?

Which reindeer is missing?" asked Santa.

"The youngest one, Santa," said the elf. "It's his first flight tonight. I've called him and called him, but..."

Just then, a young reindeer strolled up, munching on a large carrot.

"where have you been?"

asked Santa.

But the youngest reindeer was crunching so loudly that it was no wonder he hadn't heard the little old elf calling.

"Oh well, never mind," said Santa, giving the reindeer a little wink. He took out his Santa-nav and tapped in the coordinates for the Great Smoky Mountains. "This will guide us to the Great Smoky Mountains in no time."

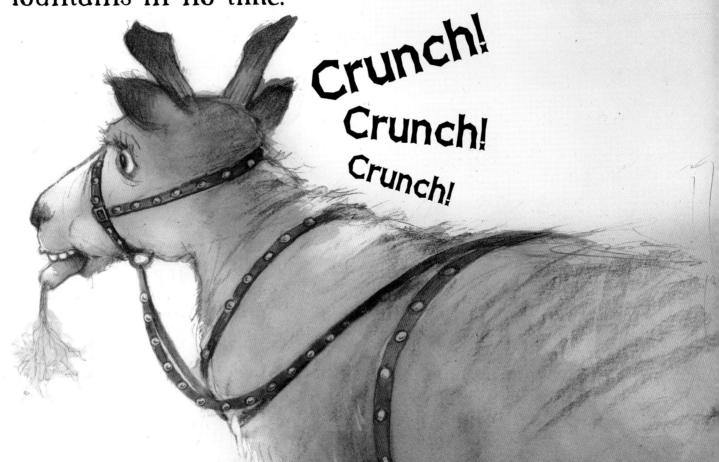

Crunch!
Crunch!
Crunch!

With a flick of the reins and a jerk of the harness, off they went, racing through the sky.

"Ho, ho, ho!"
laughed Santa.

"We'll soon have all these presents delivered to the Smokies!"

Santa's sleigh flew through the starry night, heading south across the Arctic Ocean. On they flew in the wintry air, high above Canada. In the wink of an eye, the sleigh was flying over the Great Lakes and on across Kentucky.

The youngest reindeer was very excited. He had never been away from the North Pole before.

They had just crossed Sevierville when,
suddenly, they ran into a blizzard. Snowflakes and
Smoky Mountain mist whirled around the sleigh.

They couldn't see a thing!

The youngest reindeer was getting a bit worried,
but Santa didn't seem concerned.

"In two miles..."

said the Santa-nav in a bossy lady's voice,

"...keep left at the next star."

"But, ma'am," Santa blustered, "I can't see any stars in this storm!"
Soon they were

hopelessly lost!

Ding-dong!
Ding-dong!

Then, through the howling blizzard, the youngest reindeer heard a faint, ringing sound.

Ding-dong!

He looked over at the old reindeer with the red nose. But he had his head down.

(Red nose...I wonder who that could be?!)

Ding-dong!
Ding-dong!

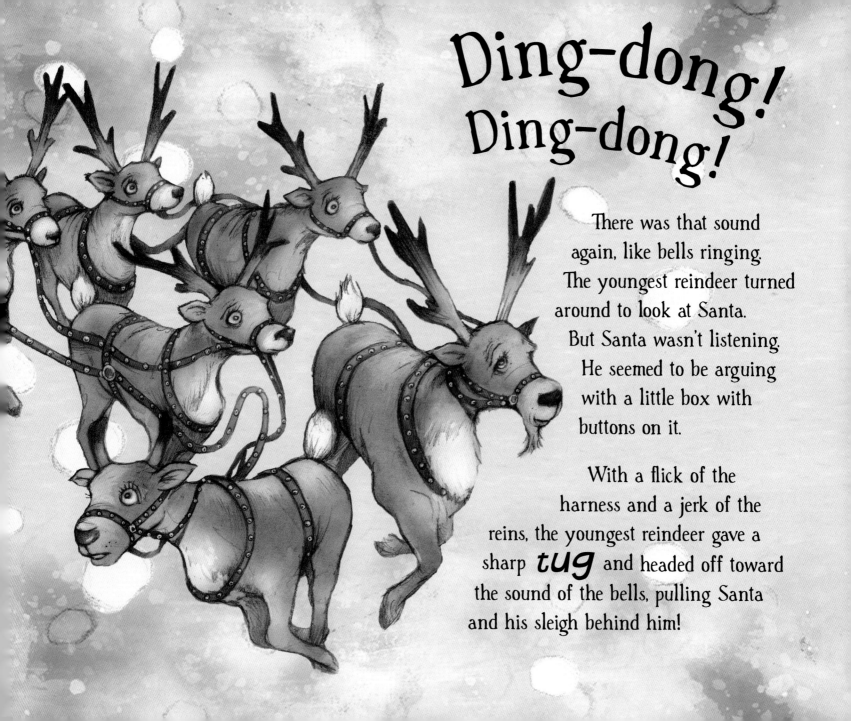

Ding-dong! Ding-dong!

There was that sound again, like bells ringing. The youngest reindeer turned around to look at Santa. But Santa wasn't listening. He seemed to be arguing with a little box with buttons on it.

With a flick of the harness and a jerk of the reins, the youngest reindeer gave a sharp *tug* and headed off toward the sound of the bells, pulling Santa and his sleigh behind him!

"Whoa!"

cried Santa, pulling his hat straight. "What's going on?" Then, to his surprise, he heard the ringing sound.

"Well done, young reindeer!" he shouted cheerfully, "It must be the bells of Sevier County Courthouse. Don't worry, children, Santa is coming!"

Then, suddenly...

CRUNCH!

The sleigh hit something as it plummeted through the snow clouds. **"You have arrived!"** said the Santa-nav unhelpfully.

Finally, when the snow had died down and the clouds parted, Santa discovered exactly where they were...

...stuck, right at the very top of a **Christmas tree** near **Sevierville City Hall!**

"Everybody, **PULL!**"

The reindeer *pulled* with all their might until, at last, with a screeching noise, the sleigh scraped clear of the Christmas tree. Santa steered them safely over Nascar SpeedPark, past Dollywood, above Ober Gatlinburg, and down into Great Smoky Mountains National Park.

Luckily, there
was no real
damage done, but
the packages had all
been jumbled up. Santa
quickly sorted out the
presents into order again.

"All right," said Santa. "Thanks
to this young reindeer I know where
we are now. Don't worry, children,

Santa is coming!"

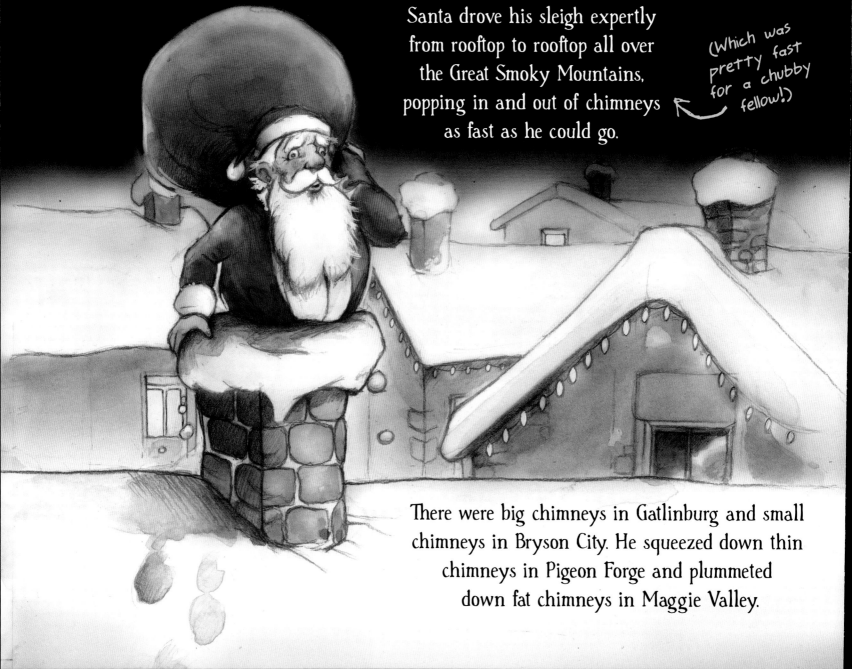

Santa drove his sleigh expertly from rooftop to rooftop all over the Great Smoky Mountains, popping in and out of chimneys as fast as he could go.

(Which was pretty fast for a chubby fellow!)

There were big chimneys in Gatlinburg and small chimneys in Bryson City. He squeezed down thin chimneys in Pigeon Forge and plummeted down fat chimneys in Maggie Valley.

The youngest reindeer was
amazed at how quickly they went.
Santa never seemed to get tired at all!
And it looked like all the children
in the Great Smoky Mountains were
going to be very lucky this year!
But the youngest reindeer was
starting to feel a bit weary
and quite hungry too!

In house after house, Santa delved
inside his sack for packages of
every shape and size.

He piled them under the Christmas trees
and carefully filled up the stockings
with surprises.

Santa took a little bite out of each cookie,
a tiny sip of milk, wiped his beard, and
popped the carrots into his sack.

In house after house, the good children
of the Great Smoky Mountains had left
out a plate of cookies, a small glass of
milk, and a big, crunchy carrot.

From Blowing Rock to Highlands, from Cherokee to Cosby, from Asheville to Knoxville, and ALL the places in between, Santa and his sleigh visited every house in the Great Smoky Mountains.

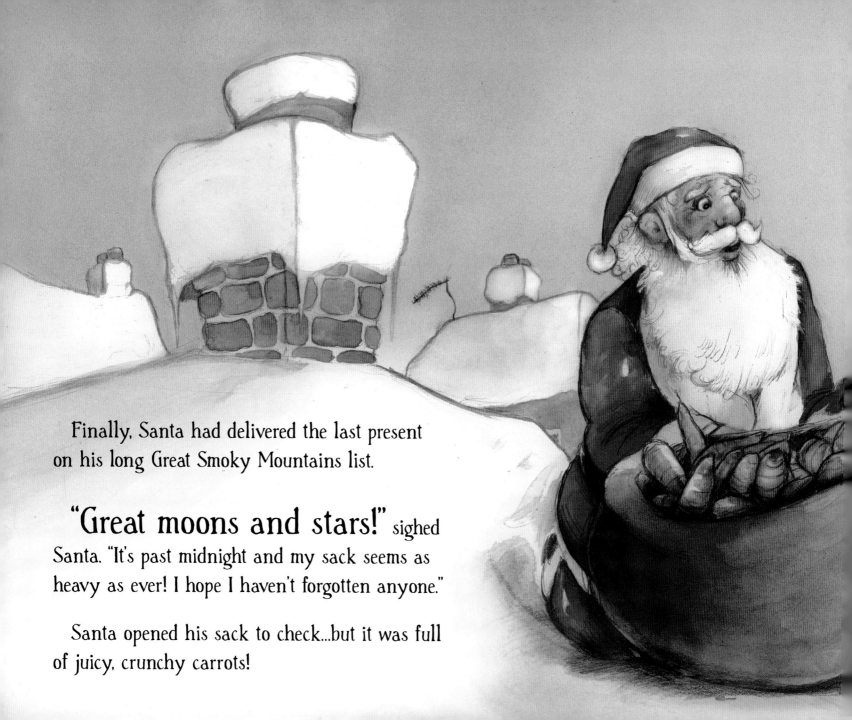

Finally, Santa had delivered the last present on his long Great Smoky Mountains list.

"Great moons and stars!" sighed Santa. "It's past midnight and my sack seems as heavy as ever! I hope I haven't forgotten anyone."

Santa opened his sack to check...but it was full of juicy, crunchy carrots!

Santa divided the carrots among all the reindeer.
"Well, done!" he said, patting the youngest reindeer gently on the nose.

But the youngest reindeer didn't hear him...he was too busy munching!

Then it was time to set off for home. Santa reset his Santa-nav once
more to the North Pole, and soon they were speeding above Mount Le Conte
and high over the Appalachian Mountains through the crisp, starry night.